Scooby-Doo and his pals from Mystery, Inc. were on vacation down under! Fred drove the Mystery Machine into the wilds of the Australian Outback. The kids were heading to a music festival at the legendary Vampire Rock.

"Wow!" Shaggy exclaimed when he first saw Vampire Rock — it looked scary!

Velma consulted her computer. "The locals call it Vampire Rock because they believe the Yowie Yahoo, an ancient Australian vampire, lives in the rock's caves."

3

The gang went in search of the music festival, which was located some-where in the woods near Vampire Rock. It didn't take long for Scooby to spot something spooky — a pair of red eyes, watching them from some bushes. Soon Shaggy saw it, too.

"Zoinks! It's the Yowie Yahoo!" Shaggy and Scooby ran and hid behind a big boulder.

"Come on, you two," Velma said, smiling. "I already told you, there's no such thing as vampires."

Scooby and Shaggy wished they could believe her. But if it wasn't true, what had they seen?

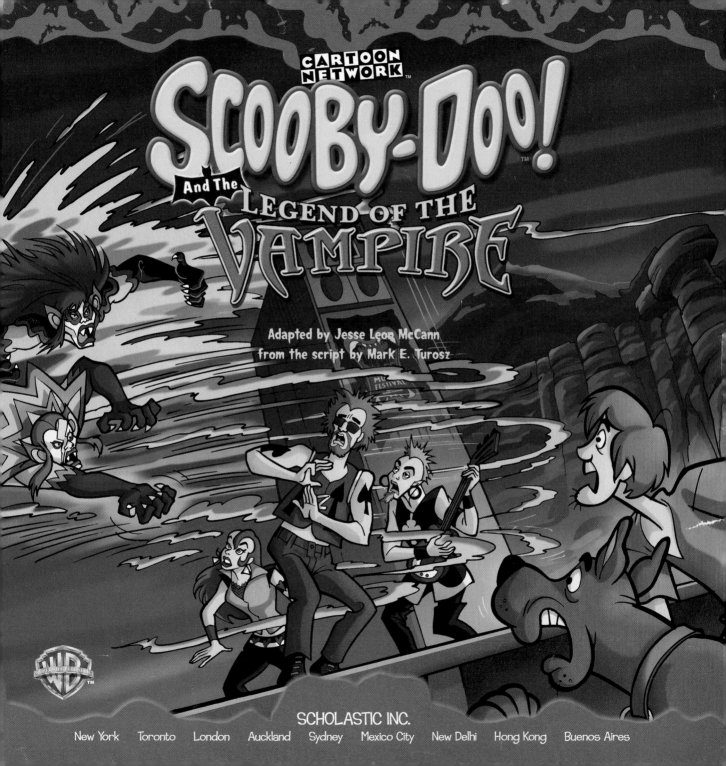

Visit Scholastic.com for information
about our books and authors online!

Cover design by Louise Bova
Interior design by Bethany Dixon

12 11 10 9 8   5 6 7/0
Special thanks to Duendes del Sur for interior illustrations.
Printed in the U.S.A.
First printing, March 2003

Just then, everyone heard a loud growl.

A pack of snarling dingoes — wild Australian dogs — appeared on the rocks above them. Then, as quickly as they came, the dingoes disappeared.

"Hey! Do you guys hear that?" Daphne could hear music now that the dingoes weren't howling.

"Come on, gang!" Fred led them along. "There must be somebody else around here."

The gang headed in the direction of the music. Soon they found themselves at the main stage of the Vampire Rock Music Festival. The stage was lit up with strobes, projections, and spotlights. More important, some old friends were onstage, practicing a song.

"Hey! It's the Hex Girls!" Daphne laughed and started dancing to the music.

Shaggy ran up to the stage. "Like, I knew those tunes sounded familiar!"

When the Hex Girls realized they had an audience, they stopped playing and squinted in the bright lights.

The lead singer, Thorn, grinned. "It *is* you! I thought the lights were getting to me."

It was a nice surprise that the Hex Girls — Thorn, Dusk, and Luna — were going to play at the music festival. They were the opening act. When Velma found out the girls had been there a few days, she asked if they'd seen anything strange since their arrival.

"Like what?" asked Thorn.

Shaggy answered, "Like, how about a big, creepy, scary . . ."

But before Shaggy could finish the question, they were interrupted by Russell and Daniel, the two guys who ran the music festival. They were worried because the Hex Girls' music had suddenly stopped.

"The finalists in our band contest keep disappearing," Russell explained sadly.

"Now more bands are quitting because another singer was kidnapped today," Daniel added.

Shaggy's eyes opened wide. "Like, maybe they were kidnapped by big, creepy, scary . . ."

A shaky voice finished his sentence. "Vampires!"

The voice belonged to a strange old man in a jeep, who started driving away. "I warned you terrible things would happen, Daniel!"

"That was my grandfather, Malcolm," Daniel explained. "He doesn't think we should have a music festival because of the Yowie Yahoo."

Daniel and Russell explained that the Yowie Yahoo had kidnapped a band called Wildwind, who had lost the previous year's contest. The Yowie Yahoo made Wildwind into his vampires, and they were terrorizing this year's bands.

"The best way to solve this mystery is to go undercover as a rock band," Fred declared. "If we're lucky, the Wildwind vampires will try to kidnap us next."

"Like, I don't want to be that lucky!" Shaggy said.

"Ruh-uh!" agreed Scooby.

The next day, the gang was onstage, dressed like a rock group. Daphne and Velma found some strange white powder on top of some amplifiers — it was glowing white makeup. Fred discovered a footprint made of a mysterious sticky, gooey substance. These were definitely clues!

Before they could do any more investigating, a golf cart pulled up to the stage. In the cart was the rock group called the Bad Omens. Behind the wheel was their manager, Jasper Ridgeway, who once managed the missing band Wildwind. When the Bad Omens saw Scooby playing the drums, they laughed.

"Why don't you amateurs take a break?" one of them sneered.

After Scooby and the gang left the stage to make way for the Bad Omens, Fred whispered, "I think we may have just met our so-called vampires."

"The Bad Omens?" asked Velma.

"Exactly," said Fred. "Jasper Ridgeway seems like the kind of guy who'd do anything to have his band win the competition."

While Scooby and Shaggy went to check out the concession stands, the others decided to investigate Jasper's plush trailer. As luck would have it, Jasper wasn't there, and they were able to sneak in.

Jasper's trailer was crowded with Wildwind memorabilia.

"There's so much stuff in here, it's going to be hard to tell the clues from the collectibles," said Daphne.

"Jinkies! I think I already found a clue!" Velma pulled a costume from inside a cabinet. "This looks just like what Wildwind used to wear."

They left the trailer, certain that Jasper and the Bad Omens were behind the kidnappings.

Meanwhile, Scooby-Doo and Shaggy were checking out the deserted concession-stand area in the best way possible — by sampling all the food! They were enjoying all sorts of Australian food and drinks laid out on a big table.

"Australians call this 'Damper.'" Shaggy held up a big piece of bread with jam. "But, like, it's not putting a damper on my appetite!"

Shaggy gobbled down the bread, then slurped down a soda. "Like, what's next, old buddy?"

But Scooby wasn't eating. He was diving under the table!

"Rampires," Scooby squeaked and pointed with his tail. The Wildwind vampires had appeared right behind Shaggy!

"Zoinks! Like, now I'm not hungry at all!" Shaggy ducked under the table, too.

Shaggy and Scooby bolted, carrying the table on their backs until they were several feet away. Soon the two buddies were running through the concession-stand area with the angry vampires right behind them!

Scooby and Shaggy ran into a tent that sold Italian food and threw on some uniforms, pretending that they worked there. When a vampire came in, they served him a big plate of spaghetti and meatballs.

The vampire forgot about the chase and looked at the plate of food with delight. Faster than even Shaggy or Scooby could have eaten it, the spaghetti was gone.

The only problem was, the vampire was now eyeing them as if he'd like to eat *them* for dessert! Scooby and Shaggy dashed away again.

Next Shaggy and Scooby fled into a tent called the House of Mirrors. Inside were fun-house mirrors that made their reflections look goofy.

Shaggy and Scooby forgot that they were running from creepy vampires when they saw their silly reflections in the mirrors. They laughed and laughed. That is, until they saw the reflection of one of the Wildwind vampires behind them. Then they cried . . . and ran away again!

Scooby-Doo and Shaggy raced back to the main stage. The Bad Omens were still practicing when Shaggy and Scooby ran through in a panic.

The band didn't know what to think. Then, while Scooby and Shaggy hid, a huge, spinning cloud appeared above the stage. Suddenly, a giant vampire emerged from the top of the swirling cloud. It was the Yowie Yahoo!

"Bwah-hah-hah-hah-hah!" the Yowie Yahoo laughed evilly.

Before the Bad Omens had time to think, the Wildwind vampires flew down and grabbed them. Scooby and Shaggy peeked up just in time to watch them all disappear, leaving the stage in a shambles. All that was left behind was a sweet-smelling smoke in the air.

Moments later, Fred, Daphne, and Velma ran up. Shaggy and Scooby told them what had happened to the Bad Omens.

"Hmmm. Well, there go our prime suspects," Fred said.

Late that night, two motorcycles pulled into the music festival campground, waking everybody up. It was a band called Two Skinny Dudes. Their real names were Barry and Harry. They laughed when Daniel told them he was glad they hadn't been kidnapped by vampires like the other bands.

"If you weren't kidnapped, where have you been?" Fred asked suspiciously.

"Exploring Vampire Rock," answered Barry, showing them his rock-climbing equipment. "We liked it so much, we decided to camp there."

"But we didn't see a single vampire," said Harry.

The next day, the gang went with Daniel to visit his grandfather, Malcolm, who was an expert on the Yowie Yahoo legend.

Malcolm was busy sending smoke signals to other members of his tribe. He used branches from a tree that grew nearby to make a sweet-smelling smoke. The same tree had a very sticky, gooey sap. Scooby found that out the hard way when he got stuck to the tree and disturbed a cranky koala bear.

"The Yowie Yahoo can only be destroyed by sunlight," Malcolm said with a frown. "You should cancel the music festival before the vampires get everyone — including you."

The gang decided the only way to get to the bottom of the mystery was by visiting Vampire Rock themselves. They climbed up a steep path and came to a rickety bridge.

"Jeepers! I knew Vampire Rock was big, but not this big," Daphne said.

As soon as everyone had crossed the bridge, they hit a fork in the path. Fred decided they had better split up.

"Zoinks! Vacation has really brought us closer together," Shaggy said nervously. "Like, it would be a shame to split up now!"

After sending Shaggy and Scooby in one direction, Fred and the girls went in another. It didn't take long for them to discover a hidden passage that led to a secret warehouse.

"Wow!" exclaimed Daphne. "I was expecting a vampire's lair to be more spooky."

There was technical equipment everywhere. It was all stuff used for rock concerts — projectors, wind machines, special-effects units, smoke machines, and sound amplifiers. The gang could tell someone had been there recently, because all the lanterns were lit. But who?

Meanwhile, Scooby and Shaggy explored the other way around Vampire Rock. Suddenly, they heard the sound of growling coming from behind them!

"D-d-dingo dogs!" cried Shaggy.

They backed away from the ferocious, snarling beasts. Unfortunately, their escape was blocked by a wall of rock and a nearby mountain pool.

"We can't run and we can't climb," Shaggy said. "Like, we need a miracle, Scoob!"

Minutes before, Daphne had gotten separated from Fred and Velma. Before long, she ran into one of the creepy vampires. It was hanging upside down from the ceiling, smiling at her.

"Jeepers!" Daphne ran down a dark tunnel that ended with a long drop off a cliff to a pool of water far below.

The vampire was right behind her. Daphne had no choice but to jump! Luckily, the splash she made frightened the dingoes away from Scooby and Shaggy. They were all saved!

"Like I said, a miracle." Shaggy smiled. "Or Daphne doing a cannonball off a cliff!"

Soon the Mystery, Inc. gang was back together again. And the Wildwind vampires were right behind them!

"We need to stay together and remain calm," Fred said, as the gang ran away from the vampires.

Just then, the Yowie Yahoo appeared out of a swirling cloud above them. He let out a thunderous roar! And the Wildwind vampires were flying through the air, swooping down in attack formation!

"Like, if there was ever a time not to be calm, this is it!" cried Shaggy.

The Yowie Yahoo opened his mouth again and giant fireballs shot out. Great blasts of flame scorched the ground all around them. Shaggy and Scooby hid as explosions of rock rained down all around them.

Then the Yowie Yahoo slammed his mighty fists together. The force of his blows shook the earth. He blew a burst of hot air from his mouth. Fred, Velma, and Daphne were almost blown away!

"Like, the Yowie Yahoo sure is full of hot air!" Shaggy cried.

Velma looked toward the east, and then back to the others. "The sun is almost up."

Fred smiled. "Vampires have to get inside, or the sunlight will destroy them."

The Wildwind vampires had disappeared, but the Yowie Yahoo stayed in the shadows of Vampire Rock and continued his attack. He was heading right for Scooby-Doo!

28

"Relp!" gulped Scooby.

Then an amazing thing happened. Just as it looked like the Yowie Yahoo was sure to get Scooby, a ray of sunlight shone onto Scooby's dog tag. The reflected light bounced off the tag and hit the Yowie Yahoo square in the chest. The giant vampire began to fade, and then it disappeared into thin air!

"Scooby, you did it!" Daphne cheered. "You defeated the Yowie Yahoo!"

Just when everything seemed like it was going to be okay, the Wildwind vampires returned to chase the gang again — in broad daylight! The sun was up and it didn't hurt them at all. The vampires chased the kids all the way back to the music festival grounds.

"Zoinks!" yelled Shaggy. "Didn't these vampires read the rule book?"

Just then, Daniel appeared to set a trap into action. He threw his boomerang and hit a rope, which released a net. They had captured the vampires!

Once the vampires' makeup was removed, they were revealed to be the Two Skinny Dudes and Russell! But that wasn't all. They were really the missing band Wildwind in disguise, seeking revenge for losing the contest the year before. Jasper was shocked that his old band was behind the big mystery.

As experts in special effects, the members of Wildwind created the Yowie Yahoo illusion with a hologram projection — which is why it disappeared when the light from Scooby's tag hit it. They used the same sweet-smelling, sticky-sapped tree branches that Malcolm had used to make all the smoke. And they used their rock-climbing gear to make it appear as if they were flying.

"We would have gotten away with it, if it weren't for you meddling kids!" muttered Russell.

That night, after the concert, Daniel's voice boomed over the speakers. "Now the winners of this year's band contest . . . the Meddling Kids!" The crowd cheered.

The Meddling Kids were a hit! The Hex Girls even joined the gang onstage as backup singers. Everyone had a great time, especially Scooby-Doo, who beat out a groovy rhythm on the drums! "Rooby-dooby-doo!" he cheered.